Fly in the Ointment

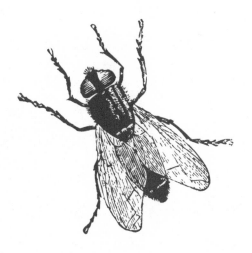

Michelle Wyatt

MICHELLE WYATT

FROM THE AUTHOR

At mid-life one has the opportunity to see the parallels, the pendulum swings, and the recycled themes bubbling up in the culture cauldron. One cannot stand and shout demands for respect, one must quietly continue working at it throughout life. Sometimes I think of myself as a has-been and in some ways a never-was, a waste of talent, a talentless quitter, a goof. Maybe these words are designed to help mitigate that, to create something, or to at least explain what's been going on between the ears. As the Sun in my own galaxy, I'm huge and powerful. I sustain life. I light the darkness. I thaw the chill. So lest this old Sun go out, I've tried to keep a sense of pride and self worth, even if sometimes displaying an unflattering portrait of a woman trying to look past the clouds to the light beyond. Some of these poems may make you laugh, cry, narrow your eyes angrily, or just scratch your head in confusion. I can't apologize for it.

Some days I walk down to the river and sit in the sun and listen to it rush by. I drink it in and imagine those 10,000 points of light. When I walk home, through spiders' webs, with apologies, I am grateful. Sometimes things don't make much sense when you look at them straight on, sometimes you have to glance at them sidelong as the mist rises later in the day than it should, where the beams cross through the mist revealing the silhouette of what was transparent, but always present.

It's the revealing that always takes my breath.

Michelle Wyatt
April 20, 2019

3

MICHELLE WYATT

CONTENTS

Fly In the Ointment

ACKNOWLEDGEMENTS

I wanted to publish a collection of poetry for the last 30 years, but I lacked the discipline to ever finish much of anything for myself, as a working adult. I had this wonderful extended adolescence in which much of my time was spent in frivolous pursuits; enjoying dance clubs, late nights out with friends, chasing adventure and love. This, naturally, turned into marriage, children, bills and the drudgery of life's logistics. The dream never died, there was simply no time to realize it. Social media became an outlet for publishign snippets of the voices I sought to bring to life. After 8 years of giving those platforms my sketches, poems, and thoughts, I have collected some of it here in these pages.

There are many people to thank and I could never list all of the influencers who brought me here. What I must do on this page is tell you about those who taught me the things I chose to carry with me. My grandfather taught me to see patterns in nature and to see everything around me as a tool to build something better. My grandmother taught me about music, how to weave beautiful words and phrases to tell a story. My father taught me how to be brave, love hard, and to "do something, even if it is wrong." My mother taught me how to persevere through pain and rise from the ruins as something more than before, for a higher love. Jim Seay, creative writing professor, along with my inspiring classmates as the University of North Carolina taught me to write poems with purpose. I think of them in Greenlaw Hall, walking out under the shade of the trees in the quad as the Carolina blue sky filtered delicately down to our tarred heels. I have to thank my friends from those years, and those since, who have supported me and have given me encouragement and sorely needed perspective. I also have to thank my colleagues in the elections community, where I have spent my career, we have seen so much change in this country and so much work is still to come.

Mostly this book would not have been possible without heartbreak and loss for it is truly in the depths of that misery, when the only sounds left to you are your own, that you can speak authentically and from a depth that resonates across generations and cultures.

Thank you, reader, as well. Thank you for reading even one of these pages. May anything I impart to you be a blessing in some way in your life.

DEDICATION

This book is dedicated to Wyatt and Georgia, the great loves of my life.
Keep the light so that you may be the light.

TRANSCEND

Blessed are the meek; for they shall inherit the Earth.
Matthew 5:5

We've been here before
That old precipice
With its sandwich board prophets
And the countdown
Unscientifically counting down.
Here we go again
When some hero emerges
And turns back doomsday
So the countdown can start
Once again and forever.

A nest of flies emerged in my kitchen.
I took my swatter, and smote the

Fly clan and wondered if they saw

A million warring angels upon them,

If I was their locusts or great beasts.

I showed no mercy because they had

That shimmery green tint you see in fields

Where cows have shat upon the clover

They were flies that bite and leave

Red circles where their fear and fury manifest.

One-quarter of my swatter is missing

I think this gives them a fighting chance

And I wonder if that is how it is with the law,

The truth we are supposed to be

Willing and able to discern.

One swat and a 25 percent chance

We live to fly again as if the threat never came.

Maybe America gets the pass this time

Or maybe this is the great righting of wrong

Whatever it is, it is not inadvertent,

We have been born and emerged

in a room in which we do not belong.

I think about opening the door

Chasing them all out where they belong

As part of ecology, where they are loved

And studied for their contribution

To shit management.

No one will open the door for us.

We will hide or we will fly, eventually tiring out.

We will study the lights and sound and

Do our best to avoid the swatter.

Our brightest will go to the bathroom

All evidence points to the dung there.

But, poised on the window of truth,

They will see each and every time,

That thing they need,

Is flushed away into the mysterious

And deadly unknown.

The large and brutish lot will come head on

To the 10,000 swatting angels.

Smote in midair, and eventually stomped

Underneath a house shoe

later flicked with a curious cat's paw

still later swept into obscurity.

There will be some stuck to the windows

Staring home, praying for the atomic

Particles to give in to their prayers

So they can slide through like shapeshifting

Shit eaters.

These are the easiest to kill.

Their belief is stubborn, they are starved,

They are tired, they accept the end
And die as martyrs.

There will be One.
This one will find a door
And wait by it in the dark
As the large and unconquerable
Beasts pass in, then out,
Eventually it opens wide
And the light and wind caress
The One's back.
A kaleidoscope of green, brown, blue, gold
Truth's fulfillment.
The promised land.
The only one who makes it out
Is the one who goes home victorious
No longer confined
To bathroom protocols,
kitchen window doctrines.

Here there is no history or future
There is only today,
you in your nature,
where you belong
in a larger world where it is easy to
See outside your own profits
And losses to the essential and

Unquestionable truth that you
Are a part of the expanding and
Contracting Universe, a 1 or a zero.

I have come to believe it's not the meek
Who inherit the Earth. Maybe that word
Was translated poorly for the King.
Or we have misunderstood its meaning.
I believe it is the patient and purposeful
Truth-loving optimists, because they wait.

If everything eventually dies
Into the earth and becomes protein for the
Beetles, who become protein for the chickens,
Who become protein for the people
Who are the prey of God and beast.
Every time.
Why fight it?

Transcend, instead.

ADVANCE

The weight of progress is its cost,
A tariff, a trade, an albatross
slung 'round the neck of those
whose open mouths can
say no other words
whose brains can
think no other thoughts.

We live in the shadow of a history
rewritten, refined, decaying--
it's stench like the rotten fruit
in forgotten gardens,
where the ant carries more than its share
back to the hill without complaining
of exploitation or wealth redistribution.

We have burns on our hands
from the tug of war.
We have blood on our hands

from the bombs and the fetuses.
We have mud on our faces,
our hypocrisy exposed,
our Freudian slips showing.
Those things we thought were inalienable?
Alien.

The sky darkens above both the wolf
and the lamb.
The rain falls on the terrapin and
the scorpion.
The offending eye is cast out of the
same head of the non-offending eye.
Trees in Africa, twenty-five hundred years
living, are dying now.
I can't tell if it's the end times, progress, or
Darwin's theory.

Some say to drink the kool-aid, stretch out
in your sneakers and leave your shell behind
so that the ship coming 'round the sun can pick you up
when the asteroid passes by.
Still others stick to the pragmatism of
the old religion's tar pit like the unapologetic
t-rex nibbling on a bronto burger before light's out.
Then, the ones who only believe the first thing
they ever heard out of their baby ears, the ones
who believe in the tooth fairy, but not the truth fairy,
wait outside the guarded gate to God's Great Garden.

Above us, angels and demons battle,
casting blows in the unseen arena.
What happens next has happened before,
the outcome is a cyclical event
and the beast, bent, makes its march
toward Bethlehem to be born
and, then later, scorned.

This age of the widening gyre
will give way to the place where the tornado's tip
touches down on the field to destroy,
sending schools, Wal-marts, trailer parks
and cows in atmospheric death swirls--
We live on the cusp of the unimaginable leap
where we will be called on to rebuild.

Be ready. Please.

THE HACKBERRIES

"Deep in their roots, all flowers keep the light."
- Theodore Roethke

I am part of the family of trees and
a descendant of this old Earth.
The mysterious moon holds nothing
I care to know with its far away aloofness.
I imagine the roots under me, destructive
and destroying, complex and natural.

I doze in the open air
On the porch with the half moon on me
There's no wind. Still, the branches
of the hackberry trees dance and swirl.
In the darkness, I can't see
the bird, squirrel or stir's perpetrator.

Without a television, phone, or person,
I breathe in the same air I have breathed
all of my life and I remember how it was

in the 1970s, on this porch, how I called
the cicadas "Watergate" bugs.
How they laughed and asked me to say it again.

I close my eyes and smell the bacon grease
of a million breakfasts, of the hairpins, the authors of
her fingerwaves. I smell his Beech Nut tobacco
evaporating in the heat on the spitting rock and
hear that same lone dog's bored barking.

Opening my eyes, I see them.

He points his finger toward the town
and grins to himself as he crosses
his legs and then his arms. She picks
dead blooms off the flowers, blows her nose,
and sticks the tissue in the pocket
of her pink housecoat.

The hugging hackberry trees turn
those ancient faces to me and say,
"We remember everything. We remember you."
The branches blow toward me and their
golden leaves fall from their underbellies
illuminated by the half moon's glow.

This is where I belong,
in this state of longing and belonging,
forgetting and recollecting,
reaping and sowing and waiting out
these years until I return, a seed.

Strom Thurmond Freeway

"... let's see how she kisses." -Strom Thurmond

I am driving on Interstate 20
on Strom Thurmond Freeway
leaving behind the worst restroom
in all of South Carolina just south
of South of the Border
and Pedro's billboards about
how one is always a "weiner" there.

I have been to Whiteville, North Carolina,
only for the day, getting up before the
cock crowed and getting home past the
enchanting hour.

Still, I have the Strom Thurmond Freeway
to thank that I got there and back in one day.

You know, they still have the ballots where
Thurmond won a write-in campaign for Senator,
one he won with his definitive rhetoric.
There's a life-size bronze of Senator Thurmond
at the Statehouse in Columbia.
Kids visit and look at it. White kids, black kids,
kids of unknown origin.
I think about Thurmond's words and deeds.
I think about his impact on South Carolina and the South.

I squint into the sun on the westward drive.
A gray fox walks to the side of the highway
curiously watching traffic whip past like
those tracers from LSD.
I wonder if he thinks we are real.
I wonder if we are.
I pull my hair back and steer with my knee,
I listen to some Skynyrd.

I like that Thurmond told Nixon to
"not use the South as a whipping boy."
I like that he defended the military and the South.
I think of every carpetbagging Yankee
who visits or invades with ideas from the North,
who waters down our tea and mucks up our barbeque,
who brags about saying "yawl," but who never ran
with bare feet across a watermelon patch carrying
Papaw a Moon Pie or a Sundrop, who

never darkened the door of a Piggly Wiggly.
We could use a little Strom Thurmond, human as he was.

I think about the debates regarding education
going on in this country and in the Great North State.
I think of my loved ones in many states, struggling
as teachers, with low pay, lack of resources and support,
with increasing demands for test scores and tolerance.
Education is everything. It is a toolbox of perspective.
It can be the difference between life and death,
a full belly and a street corner.
Our schools, our cities, all look the same.
Every city, every highway across America.
Every Hilton where I collect Honors points
has the same breakfast. There is a common core
to American life that reflects its educational imperatives.
This is the Civil Rights/Communist connection
Thurmond spoke of, and feared.

I wonder if he ever felt like that gray fox
staring into the kinetic traffic of the Civil Rights era
wondering if it was real or a psychedelic tracer.
I wonder if he felt like a hypocrite
when little Essie Mae Washington was born.
I wonder if he felt like a hypocrite
when she was just a twinkle in his eye.
I wonder if he believed everything he said.
I wonder if he believed his guidelines and
ideals applied only to the greater society
and not to bedrooms with drawn curtains
or Senatorial restrooms.

I wonder if any of them believe anything they say today.
Times, they are not a'changing, Bobby.

I put the car in cruise control on Strom Thurmond's Freeway.
I think of him losing his wife, being widowed for eight years.
I think of that pretty young thing he married when he was 66
and she was 22, that former Miss South Carolina.
She left citing a need for "independence."
I think of their beautiful daughter who died in a car accident,
only 22 when her light went out.
I think of all a person loses when they commit to public life.
I wonder why they do it.
I think of what we have lost and everything still left to lose.

I remember hearing on his last day in the Senate
his last words, "The Senate stands adjourned."
The hesitation, the waiting, the still air-- waiting,
waiting for the words to wrap up a life lived on
the southernmost high ground, The Dixiecrat.
I think of how he said, "That is all," and how
those are the most prophetic words he could have uttered.
I think of all the things I could say
all I want to say, the words confined inside
but crave their independence, their freedom.
I think of the things I want to say to you.
But there is a price for that type of freedom,
a price too high when you've seen too much and
know beyond certainty, "That is all."

February 17, 1947, a black man named Willie Earle
was lynched by 28 cab-driving white men

in Greenville, South Carolina just after Thurmond
got the keys to the Governor's mansion.
It was Thurmond who insisted on the 28 being prosecuted,
insisted on a jury that would mete out justice for his life.
But justice wasn't served and in the end, a judge
named Martin left the courtroom, his back to the jury,
without thanking them.
Even though all 28 were acquitted of any crime, Willie Earle's
was the last lynching in South Carolina,
but hardly the last lynching in the South.

A tide would turn for some--
NAACP activist Medgar Evers; the four black girls
in 1963 in Birmingham, when the church blew up;
and the 1964 slayings of three civil rights workers in
Philadelphia, Mississippi.
I know why people say "Black Lives Matter."
I think those who don't understand it should
either study some history or shut the hell up.

The bronze statue of Thurmond is neither white nor black.
Neither are stones placed in our memory, nor ash in our urns.

A freeway is not really free. It's merely a way to go.
There's a price we pay for all things; the good and the misdeeds.
We pay to live and we pay to die and along the way
we hope we have enough gas to get to love, and enough time
to find peace with ourselves for the stops we've made
and the people we've become.

THIS IS WHAT DIVORCE FEELS LIKE

Your life is less valuable to people
Than their own sense of comfort,
Than the truth.
They never want to hear you speak, I mean,
It might make the holidays uncomfortable.
In fact, you no longer exist
And neither do your children
At least while they are with you.

OK, girl.
Swallow it down hard.
It's not as if they lost your rape kit.
Because others get robbed and raped
and people forget who it even was that left you there,
The one you were shackled to, the chains cut.
"Alternative facts" have been introduced, you liar.

Years go by
you rely on whatever the latest thing is
that keeps your mind occupied.
You stay busy.
You stay hopped up
on one thing or another.
You talk mostly to people who don't know about it,
because it's easier.

Then one night you dream.
One night you dream of
an outdoor music festival and
you can't find your clothes.
You look for an old friend
who was supposed to give you
a ride home.
When you find him, you see his face
and don't recognize it.
His eyes are prison bars
that incarcerate the truth.

You wake up screaming
Divorce has altered the course of your life
in unimaginable ways.

You are frightened by the sounds
that come out of you.
They are both primal and other-worldly,
they don't sound like the woman
who accepted it all and moved on.
They sound like the cries of a victim.

You don't even care that he lives on,
happily and easily and
never considers apologizing
or explaining because it's not justice
so sorely needed here.
You must right the wrong diagnosis
that this was ever benign.

You care that you lost the brothers and sisters
but deep down they know.
Although they have victim-blamed you
You don't blame them.
You would not have done so
(at least you don't think so),
but you are not them
or him.

You care about the two graves you dug,
years ago, in the woods,
not far from where it all went down.
You care that two graves had to be dug.

You are glad they are both still empty.

The Cold Snap

It came with warning.
That didn't matter much, though, not to the chickens.
It's like one day I'm hot and smug
trying to cover up my sweat
and the next morning
I'm warming my mitts on a coffee mug.

The trees whisper predictions.
Their dried up leaves from a summer too hot and dry
tickle against one another in a type of Morse code cipher
as if to say, *"Gather it in.*
Spread the seed. Prune. Till in the garden.
Winterize.
Take them winder units out and store 'em someplace dry.
It's on its way. Don't act surprised."

The sky dresses itself in new colors.
The sun takes a new route. New stars come out.
I find myself going outside more often and see with
softened eyes the world on the verge of dying

but I don't mourn, because I know it dies
so it can again be born.

Don't believe my heart frigid
because I don't tear up while fidgeting with the work
of digging and pruning and settling in for dark days.
Although these hands may feel rough and cold,
it's only my heart that has grown old
watching these seasons unfold.

The Outfit

I went to my mother's church
for the "fall festival"
where many were dressed
in Halloween costumes.

I did not opt
to go in costume
but instead
wore one of my groovy outfits
like I would wear out
to dinner with a friend.

I was standing in line
for the cake walk
this sweet child
in front of me
turned around,
looked me up and down
and said,
"What are you supposed to be?"

I replied, "Myself.
These are my regular clothes."

She furrowed the brow
below her Cinderella crown
in disbelief, trying hard to rationalize
anyone would wear that get-up
any other day of the year.

Are You There Prufrock?

It's that time again,
to talk about forever
to talk about the road long
and life short.

To talk about the disappearing
ink in that contract you signed
for your life
before you came spiraling down
(or up, as it may be) to Earth
in your baby-soul cocoon
gurgling about living a better life
filled with more perfection
than the last.

It's time for you to scroll past
these words (and fast)
because you know at the end
you're just going to either be very
confused or feel slightly nauseous.

You know there isn't enough sand
in the Sahara to please me
and that no matter how much beauty
I can coo about today
tomorrow will be filled with righteous indignation
if the sun does not come out.

I suffer from too much of some things
and not nearly enough of others.
I suffer from the affliction of acceptance,
the malady of giving up,
which is always preceded by
the overwhelming question:
What difference does it make?

Tomorrow I may be cured.
I may be like the guru on the mountain
waving wands and sage and
drinking the elixir of the gods as it runs down
the corners of my mouth,
greasy and full of omega-3s.
I won't stop to breathe
until I pass out and "the body" takes over.

I blame too much on "the body,"
when clearly the mind and
her problematic soul
raise most of the
ruckus around here.

But she does get all of the credit.

THE ROAD

I prefer a dirt path to asphalt
a place where my feet pulse
against the ground's mulch
where the smell of earth
and centuries of decay
mix with new growth
in a sweet bouquet.

I prefer travelers in backpacks
to stiletto moms and the business class
I prefer my own beans ground
my own water pouring over them
crushed and foamed brown
to my name misspelled at Starbucks
on a size pretending to be Italian.

I prefer barter to currency,
give me a wink and a handshake
to their plastic swiping
and my fingered signing.
I would rather be here
where I know my friends

from my enemies
although they all look
the same to me.

Give me my dogs and our simple
dialogue of short commands
to the small talk of strangers.
Give me the truth of my children's day
to the monotone angels
of the GPS that define my way.
But before me is the road,
a turnpike, a toll to pay for my soul.
There is no free way.

I've had a life coach.
I heard The Secret.
I even TQMed myself out of a job
back in the 1990s.
I've been on the dirt road,
airport runways, highways,
and lost in parking lots.

I think it's strange how they all
led me here, today, to this place
from where I used to run away.

Exile

When the last words
curl from the tips
like swords of mercy
from your salty lips

When I have scrolled
back to where it began
and hung on each letter
I carved in sand

I see impenetrable bars
between our words
and miles over mountains
we failed to traverse.

So it is I stop thinking
of you in those scenes
where you laugh at my words,
we hold hands in the street.

Spring hillsides green
and the confident sun beams
its warmth like a quilt
across this valley's dreams.

And every buzzard riding
thermals in the sky
draws lines of descension,
unspoken goodbyes.

The Center Falls Out

When the wood is full
of termites and the sky
has been full of rain for days
When only faith and mold
hold it together and it's time
to replace it all and haul
the old away or burn it,

That is when the wood itself
is but a lonesome idea and
the rain but an inevitable enemy
and the sun but a revelation
in ill-placed faith in the space
of worship and warships.

It is when I listen for the cracks
in either the roof above or foundation at my feet
and trust me, I have my bags packed,
in fact, never unpacked from the last attack
of time and elementary cruelty.

But that sun stuns with its light
making all things seem possible
and the broken wheels running in the lobes
come off the spokes and fly and blind
you from behind as you fall in the Icarus path
already aware of the aftermath
for which you will not be present.

Whether it is by design and our making
or failure or some other kind,
things break and tear and wear
us down and fear may only be
fear itself, but still it scares and smears
our reputations as we crawl from the fall
in wonder of the end and all
before we, too, are gone.

I have felt the center of my own gravity fail.
I have leaned too far over the virtual rail
hoping, maybe, if I fall
it might not happen to y'all.

SHE, MAGDALENE

there's a painting of
her hair hanging down
a rock in streams like
water quenching the
thirst of humanity

you have judged her
in the darkness
you wanted her small
that woman who saw

tell me how can you
bear what is false
when it was she
saw first,
she saw God,
the apostles' apostle

you like to show a male God
forming a miniature God
from clay to lord over
human households
while looking like him

you like to write letters
legislate laws
meet with other men who

purport to know God's mind
sow fear and divide
to preserve your place
on Earth

when in fact,
it was Magdalene,
his mother, and his sister
entrusted to know him
in the womb,
as a child,
as rabbi,
as betrayed,
as slaughtered,
in burial,
in resurrection—it was they
chosen to see
and destined to tell

did it hurt his men to know
it was her eyes
He chose to see Him
first that morning
and their acts
destined to betray him
deny him
because God knows
our nature

after all the squabble
over eternal placement
this one, that one
at the right or left hand
did it break their hearts
insult their egos
that it was she,
he entrusted to see
and believe

when men hid from men
and sat amongst themselves
congratulating themselves
on their courage
speaking of power and
influence and its cost
she opened her eyes
and fixed them on Him

I think He knew
centuries of editing
would never change
the eternal fact
She was first witness
to the faith you claim.

ANTIDOTE FOR A BROKEN HEART

They are fire, people,
with their feelings and needs
and I am an empty bucket
without water or feed in it.

I think at times it's better
to have never loved at all
than to have loved so much
and lost it, and thus, this wall.

A wall I am too short to climb
my arms too weak to lift me over
What's left of me hides
beneath this wordy cover.

Maybe it's hard to understand
It's so hard to begin again.

This is the reason heart choices
are ever made in the brain.

These methods I use to avoid pain,
you may be wary of them.
Feel free to use them if you choose to,
but your mileage may vary.

ICE STORM

I have this idea
that what's happening to the planet
is happening inside me.
They call it global warming
and cast warnings
I have seen the glaciers melt
and eyeing them
have imagined melting with them,
slowly, then suddenly breaking.

I've always liked people who were hard
to like, who didn't like me,
who didn't have the capacity to match
my enthusiasm.
I imagine it as two fronts in the atmosphere,
and a wigged out meteorologist
explaining what happens when this cold front
and this warm front converge.
But the biggest mistakes I've made in this life
are ones of underestimation

of the potential of others to do harm
or good.

I'm not a bread and milk buyer
when such predictions are made.
I like to wait until the situation is dire
before going my own way.
And even then, I am often, too late
for safe passage.

How can something so numbingly cold
be so dynamic?
These ice storms are something else.
They defy logic, reason.
They coat everything with their chill,
like some sociopathic lover
who shows up after the gaslighting
to cool his hands on your winter skin.

I am still a child who believes
my own snow angel is a sign of things to come.
I believe in Spring
with her tiny shoots and songbirds
whose wings will criss-cross this river valley
like easy strokes of a pen
signing away the farm
and leaving us here to pack our bags
for Florida.

GREENER PASTURES

My words
like ripples
on the surface
of some enormous
and rocky river
and them big catfish
swimming on the bottom
live in the bosom
of my beating heart.

My desires are like herds
of grazing mammoth
insatiable and clearing
the landscape of whatever
good could have come
had it not been consumed
by large beasts with their
starving mouths.

It is a number of things
one of which is my broad love
of hyperbole and story-telling,
another of which is fatal distractions
of shiny things that sparkle in light,
yet another is my feeling I've used up
all of my second chances and am well
into thirds or more.

I suppose I tap my fingers to borrowed time
and live off what has already been spent.

So you think you know
from peering into this keyhole
all there is.
But it is not all.
Far, far from it
Far from the shoreline
far and into the wake of larger things
that toss and bury us and pass
as we sink.
We go down with our eyes open
counting "one, two, three"
and have that underwater tea party.

I don't memorize the tides
that abide by the bodies of our heavens.
And this is why
I also sink deeper than ripples
too far from shore
to rise again and call out.

It is why I accept
the inevitable
and undulating truth
that I am due miracle moments
and tragedies; peace and conflict.
It is why when I think of you
I wonder which moments you will ride in
and ride out on.
If it will be daybreak
or dusk when you go and come,
come and go.

It is why I practice skipping stones
on the ripples you have made.
It is why I imagine them tumbling
I also imagine them resting at the bottom
covered by time's dirty floor
picked up and spit out by them catfish
occasionally.

It is why I sit here on the shore
avowed to not drown
in unlikely events,
greener pastures.

All That's Left

When you look past the ornamentations
and crystal balls
past the fabrications, lies of a nicer name
And dig deep into the marrow
carving out with fingernails of scythes,
and there you look past and beyond
and then farther still
past where any wave ever broke
past where any pebble ever skipped
past the point in the ozone
where even its hole is but
an inconsequential blip.

It is there you'd see the same thing,
the unfortunate twin that turns in crude turmoil
in the center of your very own pot.
You'd recognize it, 'though you'd pretend to not,
in its black vacuum, what some call the Truth and
what others call the Devil herself.

It's like a pile of texture-free ash, without conscience,
or consequence, without grief, without one mica-thin sliver of hope.
It's the waste pile where you gave up or gave in,
sold out or broke the record for diminishing wins,
burned out or threw water on the flames of your desire.
It is the place where you said, "It doesn't matter. Not now."

It's a leafless tree, full of holes,
as simple as the wind
yet calculus complex like whom you call
a friend of a friend.

It is nothing the eye can see.
It is a thing you will deny while taking into
your lungs with every breath.
It's opposite you can say over and over
and over again trying to convince yourself
(and others) as to its validity.
You can put on a tuxedo made of its antithesis,
post pics of yourself wearing it
grinning your grimace against the wind of
your own constitution.
Yet, it will not be denied.

At some point, you grow old
The pressure grays you
Puts a permanent furrow
in your brow.
The old tricks stop working
and you can't keep your finger
in the hole in the dam above your made-up
crazy town any more.

It's then that the questions come.
The contingencies.
It's when you go to the barn
and try to fire up an old engine.
When you grapple for straws
and crawl down to darkness in
places looking for something
in your world that still works.
Something you can ride out of town.
Something you can pretend was
all you wanted all along.
Something to point to,
someone to blame,
It's a difficult thing
when you are all that's left.

Realizing that you are part of
the bigger lie puts you one step
closer to the Truth.

Realizing no one can forgive you
for delivering that box of steaming shit
wrapped with a bow until you confess
puts you one step closer to redemption.

Realizing the thick, cold, dark places
inside you are actually part of the
everlasting they dress up in psalms
and cast out with holy water brings
judgment worthless to the one judged
as redemption is futile.

We are all the same
Ghost in this machine,
Fly in this ointment.
And when we're gone
all that's left
is all that ever was.

The Only Way Out is Through

You will survive, live,
love, and prosper.
This is not the end.
Be brave and love yourself
love enough to cover the wound,
so it will heal and not consume.

Love is the ointment.
And the band-aid.
And the cells repairing underneath.
If you can love yourself and others too
(without needing others to validate you)
You'll wake up one morning and you'll be through.

THE TOOL SHED

I wince
It's a disaster
A dust-filled
Box of memories
Of projects
Abandoned
Of promises
Not kept
Of lives
Over.

Two weeks ago
I ventured inside
Looking for some
Scrap wood.
The exterior was
Compromised
The sky was visible
through its shallow ceiling.
The smell of
Sawdust and neglect
was all around.

I remember when
the "West Wing"
was built onto the shed
to house my grandfather's
John Deere riding lawnmower.
I can remember watching him
Meticulously roll it out
and roll it in
and sweep the ramp off
so there would be
not one errant blade of grass.

The ramp;
the one he made,
the one that rots there now,
enjoyed a pristine threshold
long ago.

Last year there were
woodworking projects
underway.
The shed was a storehouse
of shared dreams of
a skater and his father.
An old sander and saw
and a lonely sawhorse
remain with the scraps
I'm too heartbroken
to throw out.

I don't know when my heart
Became like that old shed.

It's like one minute
it was standing cleanly
with no cobwebs or damage
and another minute
I'm contemplating having the
Whole damn thing hauled off.

It's when things lose function
and are no longer cared for,
A reflection more on the caretaker
than the thing itself,
Decay greedily claims it all.
I have become a poor tender
to my memories and the things
around me that should function.
I have turned away dreaming,
instead, avoiding the work
and commitment it would
take to mend
or begin again.

I can't have a building
a vessel of time
a portal of truth
looking like that
in my backyard.

And yet,
I can neither fix it
nor live without it.

Yard Junk Love

I thank the Universe
for GPS and the 3rd choice
of suggested routes
sending me on back roads
to receive messages
and metaphors.

Today's message is:
Love is like yard junk
Slowly decomposing
in the weeds.

It's an old rusty station wagon
that spent years gracing highways
to beaches and ball practice
carrying a family
groceries
things from Lowe's
or trips to a Grammy's house
carrying gifts they couldn't afford
to places they can never go back.

I saw it there
peeking out from above
cinder blocks
a grill smiling through the vines
and I wondered how it got there
and why they don't see it any more.

It was once new
maybe even in a showroom
and people had a dream and bought it
probably sat in it when they picked
up fast food that first night
and carefully ate
in the new car
so careful not to spill.

But the first spill came
and then she got sick
or he lost his job
the kids grew up and left
and it may have been something
as simple as a transmission
or an alternator
or (God forbid)
a battery.

And it sat in that spot
where it's been
a long time.

Every day he saw it
and it reminded him
he should fix it
He should do something to repair it.
Or haul it off.
But he never did.

And the ice storm came and that limb fell
and cracked the windshield.
And then the cat got in
clawed up the upholstery
And the wasps built in there
And in the end it was far gone
Too far gone
To ever grace a highway
Or carry a family.

She tried to plant some pansies last year
in planters made of its old tires
But she got tired
And the bags of dirt are still there
And the pansies never even made it
Out of their tiny, black cups
into the promise of that round
new found home.

Some people drive by and wonder
why they don't clean that up
that eye-sore.

It is a surrender
publicly displayed

An admission
of failures
A challenge
never met
A memory
not worth keeping well
Left in the elements
to rust
to remind
the rest of us
we're not far behind.

THE SEARCH FOR JOY IN AMERICA
(PART 1, THE EPIPHANY)

Is it not the same wind in your face
Whether you're at the helm of a yacht
Or some little canoe thing?
The same salt air blowing 'round your head
The same fish swimming beneath
Isn't it enough to be human?
Instead of human with so many things?

Whether you're holding a sign
Asking for more, from a factory
the banks, the government or a store--
It perplexes me the same as the CEO
With the toilet of gold
Who flushed his company profits
Into the sewer below.

Sometimes the Great Mother Nature,
(whatever you want to call her)
Sends a cyclone, tornado, or
Quakes the ground to shake the mound
that sits above our shoulders
and beneath Her eyes.

As if to say, "All that matters
is your gray matter. And the air.
And love." Then she takes from
the quakes and shakes from the
greedy mistakes (like 9/11 and w a r)
and if to say, "Hey. Now that you're at
ground zero, everything's going to be okay."

I have never understood the art of coveting
I don't want what you have
I don't dream about dancing through your
beautiful kitchens, beach houses, wearing
your designer jewelry and pricey blouses.
I was your neighbor I heard what you think,
and I said, "Get me out of here."

Maybe your biggest beef is with the "deadbeats"
and not with me. Because your tax money
never fed me or my family, honey.
But you're still a little miffed because I don't want
To spend, to acquire, to flaunt.
I'm sorry, but I just don't.

It's bitter cold today in this old house.
I walked down to my chicken coop.
I gathered eggs, fed them, brought their water
(frozen solid) up to the house.
The wind bitterly blew against my lips and I felt them chap
And I celebrated that moment as the sun rose
To be alive and human and worthy of prose.

TAKE COVER

Cover your insecurity
With a flag-like blanket.

Keep it simple, Stupid.
Don't say anything that might
Put you out there
Make people talk in hushes
Roll their eyes into
Their facepalms
Sip a drink that cost more
than your MAGA cap.

Eschew the hipsters
With their randomness like
Scattered seeds, predictably
blowing beyond your wall.
Dislike their petulant smug
Their far-fetched ideas
(which are the same ideas you
had 40 years ago)
The impossibility of their

approval on a loan for
that vintage Airstream.

Assume that everyone is
An imbecile except you
and the others wearing your colors.
Predict who's most likely
to succeed in tearing down
Everything that means
Anything to you
Tell them over and over and over
how wrong they are.

But you'll waste your breath
(you might need it one day
so save it).
You might as well
Get into a phone booth with a bear
(as if there are any more phone booths
for the increasing bear population)
and apply sandpaper to its hind haunches

Wrap your head in the flag too.
But be careful not to make it
look too turban-like.
Alert the agents running
the TSA radiation scanner
the day after the day some
Guy said the world was going to end.

As for me, I don't have
Any answers for you at all.

I live by what I feel after
Living as many years as you.
My flag doesn't look like yours.
I made it with all of
the leftover colors in the box
crude drawings of the saints,
Now dead, but not silent.
None of whom would mind
if I left it somewhere
Or burned it.
(Because they know the Truth.)
One must be careful of
flags with rules,
hipsters in Airstreams,
assumptions about a world
that changed while you
were taking your selfie,
and poems that do not rhyme.

You see, while your dogs
barked, wildfires raged.
While your biopsy results
were mailed,
That child in Lumberton was
abducted and killed.
While your biscuits burned
I wrote these words.

No one will remember details,
at least not well.
We can leave the lion's share
of responsibility

to the US Supremes,
The Texas Board of Ed,
and Donald J Trump
(details redacted and left in a
Miss Universe contestant's
make-up bag).

Your flag is old and dusty
and the stories it tells
fail to evoke one iota of
wistful nostalgia in me
nor promise a good night's
sleep.

It is the security of my resolve
that keeps me stuck to the
underbelly of this flat earth.
And in that way, we are
inarguably
the same.

ODE TO AMERICA

America, don't be confused by my words ever again.

I love you true
with your flying flags
gun salutes
helicopters full of strong men
jumping out and running headfirst into trouble.
I love those men and women
who forfeit personal independence
so I can make comments
and go wherever I please.
I do not love to hear
they have died or been held captive.
I do not love to hear
they have tortured or been tortured.
But America, I do not understand where war ends
and bullying begins.

I love election day
with the electioneering shouts
and complaints of voters
of intimidation
or suppression
always both.
I do not love the masses
who never vote
unless some fool
Or guerilla marketing
gets them lathered up.
I do not love the dollar
dictating who will win.
It's supposed to be us.

I love the waving reeds on the coast
and the thick forests in the west
I love the mountains
and the fields.
I do not love the water
Bubbling with poison.
I do not love the oil
that coats the wings
Of birds.
I do not love how the
so-called independence of some
summons death for others.

I love your history, America,
full of stories of people
who did the right thing
always not the popular thing.

I love the men with good posture
and the ladies who knew how to
sew or trek or configure underground
railroads.

I love how men talk of victory
and women talk of occupation.
I do not love how no one knows
how they are going to withdraw
And leave the war party.
I do not love how history gets
rewritten and generations
come of age not knowing
the truth, the whole truth,
nothing but clickbait.

I do not love the corporations.
They are the anti-Democracy.
They operate with only a single
consciousness--
preserve the corporation
at all cost to life, human or otherwise.
Corporations have the freedom to
avoid taxes or exploit a workforce.
Contrary to our high court
Corporations should not have
the same rights as us,
the free people, to donate to
political campaigns.

I love you, America, I love you true.
Some say because I don't

support foreign or domestic
Gun murders that I'm not a patriot.
Some say because I don't
like invading foreign countries
because some guy says it is a last resort
means that I should not be
part of any discussion.
I have been called "ignorant libtard"
"Dreamer snowflake,"
And a "Threat to national security."
And to that I can only shake my head.

I was made in America.
In this day, at this time
I am a product of her unobstructed rearing--
her public schools, public university,
public parks, public beaches,
I was her public servant for 15 years.
And I don't need a private school politico,
Fox Media mogul, red pill revolutionary,
or corporate international
to announce that I am
un-American.

I am the salt of her earth
Love child of her womb
by her people
for her people
With liberty
And justice
For all.

THE PURSUIT'S THE THING

My dying thoughts should be
of mornings such as these:
Coffee on the front porch with
Wyatt and Georgia
waiting for the bus,
throwing oversized sticks to Oz,
cuddling Ginger like a baby
and telling twisted stories in that
dog-diva voice I imagine is hers,
listening to the older roosters
demonstrate their crowing prowess
to the younger ones as they try.

Waving them off, saying
"I love you! Have a great day!"
as the kids go to the bus
and traverse realms where
I do not belong.

Curious, so curious,
how beautiful the mundane
we take for granted.
I can't imagine how I landed this life
with its unspeakable tragedies
and high comedies
woven with scenes like this one--
roosters crowing,
dogs putting on a show,
my family talking about
the refugee crisis and
bad jokes while the cats stare
out the storm door
at a breeze no one else sees.

I recently thought I'd lost
the ability to love,
as if it had been cauterized
from my heart.

But this *is* the way I love--
these people,
these creatures,
on the porch
under the light
where hornets are building a nest
I dare not disturb,
because the cold comes
soon enough,
I've learned.

Let them build in their tireless pursuit
without a future.
In that way,
they aren't so different
from the rest of us.

Mr. Godman, The Party Is Over

The party is over.
Go on now.
It has changed,
Aged,
shifted.
The "rape train to success"
won't be leaving the station anymore.

I don't spend my free time
arguing
morality and politics
with people these days.
People with lives full
Of tawdry tales,
their lies and
Sexual deviancy.
If you saw their browser history
Or parked a drone outside
The window to their room
You'd blush
Even if you belong to
A swingers club.

The Great Morality is freedom,
Mine and yours.

I don't care what you do
With one exception:
Don't take your hypocrisy too far
When you wear it out and
We all know firsthand who you are.

This is the revolution,
Humanity's original sin,
The lie they have told on God.

A giant man in the sky
making that insignificant little helper
out of the rib of the
easily-influenced little god man.
The way they tell it is
God's little narcissism project
was lonely and needed help
So God took a rib
And factioned woman out of it.
Things were going well, too,
except she ruined it all
With her lack of self-control.

God did not make you
Your mama did.
If she is still living,
she knows more about your soul
than you do.
If she is gone,
a part of you is gone.

Generations have eyewitnessed
their mothers' beatings.

They have seen them work
as maids,
in factories and mills,
waiting tables,
Then coming home,
cleaning until her back broke
and yes, staying,
when it was not safe to stay,
to give them shelter in the storm.

They've seen her count her coins
while Mr. Godman goes and gets his
because he "works so hard."
They've heard her cry
and sensed the fear and futility
of how it feels to love someone
and need someone
who dishonors the vows,
who disowns truth,
who gaslights,
Who uses and destroys.

They have seen their mothers try
to pull together a meal because
"we don't get paid until tomorrow,"
they have seen who left
and who stayed
and who sacrifices every stinking day
and who gazes all week into his own
God-like image.

They've come to us
Their mothers
time and again for renewal.
We Are The Source,
The fountain on the mountain.
Do not deny it with your lying.

The big lie was bad enough
To bring on the revolution.
We are generations into injury on insult.
We know our worth
the power suffocated
from our burning lungs
Burning as we held our tongues
to avoid upsetting
The One Who Works So Hard,
the One in whose image
God himself was made.

Mr. Godman and his sycophant band
say the words so matter-of-factly at the church,
at the office, at Thanksgiving,
in your bedroom--
you have apologized every day
up til now for Eve and all,
And you agree
the fellas have it bad
and it's the same thing
with the same name.

Where, oh where is daddy,
Mr. Goodbar,
Daddy Warbucks,
and Indiana Jones when you need them?
Make sure they all know
you are on the team with high-T
even if it means you need to shut up
and look pretty while you vote
Against your own freedom.

Listen here, you and I
don't live in the same world
if that's your geisha act.
If you can't see the
Systemic
Institutional
Cultural
Historic bias,
Someone has certainly gouged out
Your pretty little eyes.

I'm not saying
Men need to wear pink
march for the women
do the dishes
or put the spray and wash
on their skidmarks once in a while--

I am saying, "look at it and see it.
Internalize it.
Then, live your life

every day
from now until you die
without rewarding or
accepting sexism anywhere,
in any capacity."

The coronation into forever
Will no longer be attended
By those 40 virgins—
Even heaven knows this is the revolution
humankind has been staving off
and whose time has come.

When you look back on this moment
years from now,
girls and boys,
you will be ashamed to admit
if you were,
(after centuries and centuries
of the most obvious wrongs
hindering progress
and threatening human existence),
still trying to apologize to him
and for him.

REGRET

My freedom is a forgotten pet,
gone without food and water for so long
she's fallen sideways
with rigor firmly set in.

Now I know why old people
shake their heads at youthful freedom.
Jealousy. Regret. Defeat.
If she was alive at all,
I'd apologize to her.

I'm going to have to stop
standing by her cage
and reminiscing like this.
It's not healthy.

VISION

Hindsight
is the true gift
of motherhood.

If it all seems so familiar,
it's because you're walking in circles.

THE WALL

What separates you from others
and binds you tightly down
to its narrow way
will not allow you
to experience freedom.

It is freedom's opposite.

When I Criticize America

When I criticize America,
I'm not being unpatriotic.
I'm trying to help a sister out.

It's like how I would
tell a friend to get help
with a rodent problem
in her home.

"You seem to have a bit of a rat problem, my friend."

I'm not saying her house is awful
or that she is a terrible person,
I'm just saying,
"you have rats running around,
it's a problem. Do you want me to call
a pest control service?
I got this thing at Ace Hardware
you plug into an outlet that emits
a sound they don't like
and it seemed to work."

I think it would be worse to pretend
that my friend doesn't have a rat problem
and she gets sick.
If I just didn't say anything,
I wouldn't be much of a friend.

Say something.
This is how it works.

RELATIVE

To the Cherokee, the black bear
was one of their children who
turned wild in the forest.

Walk in these woods today
and you will hear ancient drums
beneath the trees
and the plink of creek rocks
like banjo strings.

Winter's freezing fog and
shroud of clouds can make
you question your choice
to live here.

The turkeys agree, especially the ones
left solo to fend for themselves.
The winking newt rests on the
precipice of eradication,
but winks anyway.

Turkey vultures roost on my chimney.
I feel a kinship with these.

They jump to the deck to eat
the kibble my dogs leave behind.

Winter doesn't last forever, I say aloud.
Soon after this time, there will be
more salamander orgies, rain,
the patient toad that waits for me
at night by the steps.

There will be more squirrels, and
their hoarding, descendants of
my grandfather's squirrel, Charlie.
I think hoarding nuts is okay if
that's what the trees are giving you.

I'm not going to argue over
over the placement of cloths
on the heads of men and women
That's their business.
I'm not going to argue over ancient texts
or science, an attempt at truth
on a physical scale
or religion, an attempt at truth
on a metaphysical scale.

I won't be used
shamed
categorized
by irreverent and sarcastic memes.
I won't be part of a cult that divides

humanity from its history or its heart
or especially its people.

Even the Cherokee forgot the prayers
they were to say, in reverence
and were wooed by European fur traders.
The chiefs, Bear and Wolf,
sentenced their brother Cherokee to disease.

Even so, the plants were kind
and gave themselves as medicine,
nature's compromise and gift.

Did you know tadpoles from frogs
eat unborn toads in river's wet pools?
There is nothing pro-life about that.

Mountain lions no longer live here,
they say, but I have seen one with my eyes.
The Cherokee did not know, at the time
that the disease came walking off the ships.
They blamed themselves for breaking
the pact with the animals.
Where blame is placed tells more
about the accuser than the accused.

We are counseled to compromise.
All of life is this ongoing series
of compromises that ends in hoarding

or disease, tourist towns or cautionary tales,
a path on course, or a trap.

The white disease killed half of them
before their organized death march
where broken, brown-skinned people
with nothing sought a new home.
Their ghosts are not in Oklahoma,
but march toward us still--
to see if we ever learned anything.
Anything at all.

When history's documents reflect words
like "eradicate the race from earth,"
there is never and will never be
any justification for it.
Some lived, and they were those who
escaped to these mountains and
still live in our blood
as the antidote.

These mountains are the children
of Creation, violently born of thrusting
plates, hot lava, and later, erosion.
They have seen the comings and goings
of ice ages and bison.
Far greater forces than us shaped this place.

So don't tell me about your God
Or your politics.
Ask me if I can still love others.
Ask me if I can live with myself.

Ask me if I can think for myself.
Ask me if I am kind.
Then ask yourself the same.

Any words someone told you
or you heard on opinion news
is propaganda I cannot accept.

Any words they tell you that fit into a bite or byte
reflect a sliver of truth so small it may as well be a lie.

I found a stone last week
that looks identical to one
found in Morocco last year.
The hellbender living in these mountains
is proof we were Asia and Asia was us
in Pangea.
Who are we to say what is ours?
None of it is.

When we extinguish people, we seal our fate.
Gray graves will always be.
The American toad can sense chemicals in the water
and not lay its eggs there.
The same is not true for the American.

We are like the tortoise who moves too slow
to know the forest's topography so we believe
every stick and every leaf an authority on trees.

Across a parking lot my own two cubs
lumber toward me, laughing,

about how I am on time for once.

The teases sting a little
A small pain that eases when I see their faces
full of the wisdom of Nature and
the alchemy of Spring.

ATLAS

I enjoy looking at the world
This way
Without satellite
Or street view.

Paper
Smells like curiosity
The colors and lines sacred
Renderings of places
My ancestors
Or I traveled.

Granny would delegate
Delicately, "We are here,"
then trace the lines
to the places
We would go.
The reds, greens, and tans
A greater authority
A surer representation
Of a truth we could

All agree on
More often than not.

Same is true for navigating
Political landscapes
What was is in stark contrast
To today's chaos
Of knowing too much.

We are the atlas
Narcissistically mined
And mapped,
A lost and sacred art
A waste of time until
Alien, AI, Angels
Water or Fire
Decide enough is enough
Of this people phase.

What are they waiting for?

I hope the storm comes
Or the meteor
And we see in the looking glass
The terror we have inflicted on Earth
And each other.

We need symbols,
Representations for guidance.
I want to be more like the atlas
And less like the live stream.

We need to realize
We are not all cut out
For a mission
an expedition
or the operating room.

ABOUT THE AUTHOR

Michelle Wyatt spent most of her career working in US elections in product development/technology and marketing. Michelle holds a BA in English from the University of North Carolina at Chapel Hill. Michelle has compiled some of her favorite writings in this book for her friends, both present and future.

Michelle's writings reflect her life at home, her upbringing and surroundings, nature and family. Her voice tells a story both spiritual and political, using nature itself as the metaphor.

Made in the USA
Monee, IL
19 July 2021